* A CORRUPT FORM OF COMPANY AS THE EAST INDIA COMPANY WAS KNOWN.   ** ALLOWANCE

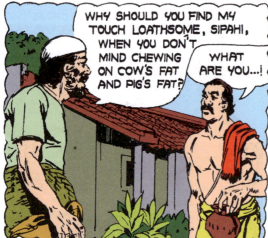

* CAMP FOLLOWER OR TENT PITCHER

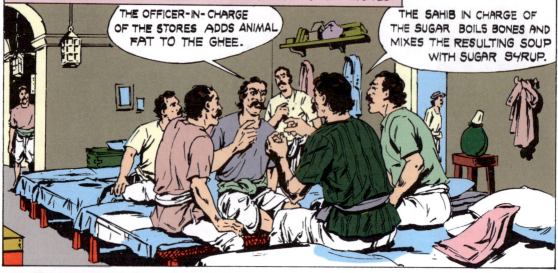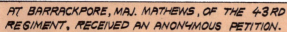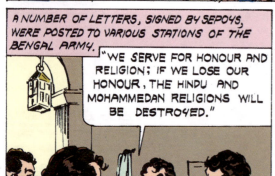

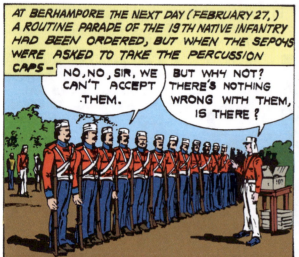

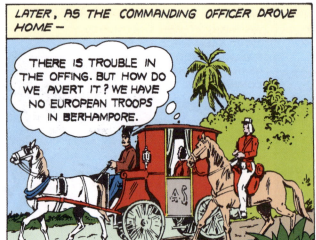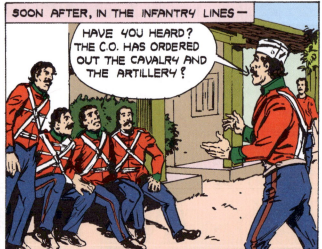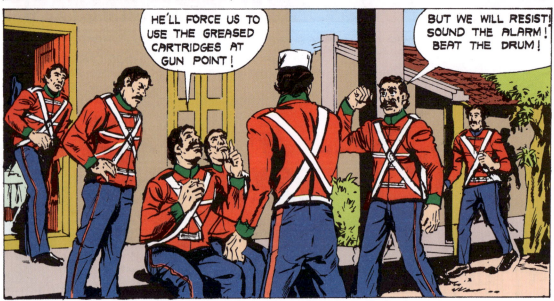

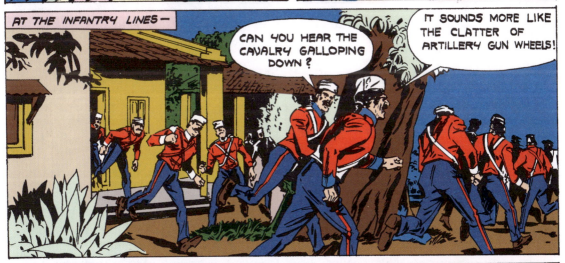

THE SEPOYS HEAVED A SIGH OF RELIEF WHEN THEY HEARD THE TRUNDLING SOUND OF ARTILLERY MOVING AWAY AND THEY SAW THE CAVALRY TORCHES MOVING FURTHER AND FURTHER AWAY INTO THE DARKNESS. THEY KNEW THEY WERE SAFE FOR THE MOMENT.

THE NEXT DAY, THE 19TH NATIVE INFANTRY FELL IN FOR PARADE AS IF NOTHING HAD HAPPENED. PERHAPS THEY HOPED THE INCIDENT WOULD BE OVERLOOKED.

BUT IT WAS NOT TO BE. A COURT OF ENQUIRY WAS HELD. TO THE BRITISH ARMY AUTHORITIES IT WAS CLEAR THAT THE 19TH NATIVE INFANTRY WOULD HAVE TO BE DISBANDED.

THIS WORRIED THE GOVERNOR-GENERAL IN CALCUTTA.

"IT IS EASY TO DECREE DISBANDMENT, BUT HOW DO WE ACCOMPLISH IT WITHOUT THE BACKING OF EUROPEAN FORCES?"

"THAT'S TRUE, LORD CANNING. OTHER NATIVE REGIMENTS MAY MUTINY IN SYMPATHY."

"I WILL GET BRITISH TROOPS FROM RANGOON. WE WILL ANNOUNCE THE VERDICT ON THE 19TH N.I. AFTER THE BRITISH TROOPS ARRIVE."

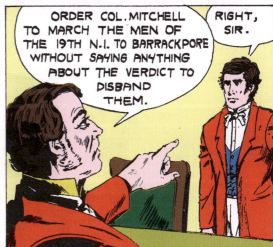

"ORDER COL. MITCHELL TO MARCH THE MEN OF THE 19TH N.I. TO BARRACKPORE WITHOUT SAYING ANYTHING ABOUT THE VERDICT TO DISBAND THEM."

"RIGHT, SIR."

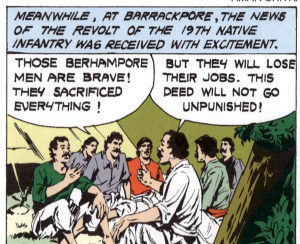

* GOVERNMENT

* LT. BAUGH.

* FOREIGNERS

BUT IT WAS NOT TO BE AS HE HAD HOPED. MANGAL PANDE DID NOT DIE; HE WAS SEVERELY WOUNDED.

SOME DAYS LATER, HE WAS TRIED. HE WAS ASKED WHO HAD INCITED HIM TO MUTINY, BUT HE REFUSED TO SQUEAL.

I ACTED OF MY OWN WILL.

HE WAS SENTENCED TO DEATH AND, ON APRIL 8, 1857 MANGAL PANDE, WAS HANGED IN THE PRESENCE OF THE WHOLE REGIMENT. RETRIBUTION HAD COME SWIFTLY.

ISHWARI PRASAD, HEAD GUARD, WAS SENTENCED AND EXECUTED ON APRIL 21. IT TOOK THE BRITISH GOVERNMENT FIVE WEEKS TO DECIDE ON WHAT PUNISHMENT TO METE OUT TO THE OTHERS. FINALLY IT WAS DECIDED THAT THE REST OF THE 34TH NATIVE INFANTRY SHOULD BE DISARMED AND DISBANDED.

THEY WERE STRIPPED EVEN OF THEIR UNIFORMS. BUT THEY WERE ALLOWED TO KEEP THEIR KILMARNOCK CAPS WHICH THEY HAD THEMSELVES PAID FOR. THESE THEY TRAMPLED UNDERFOOT, CONTEMPTUOUSLY.

WHO WANTS TO KEEP THE CAPS? LET THEM HAVE THOSE AS WELL!

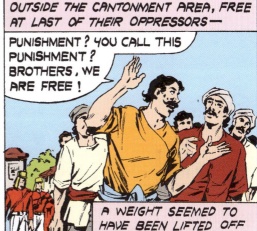
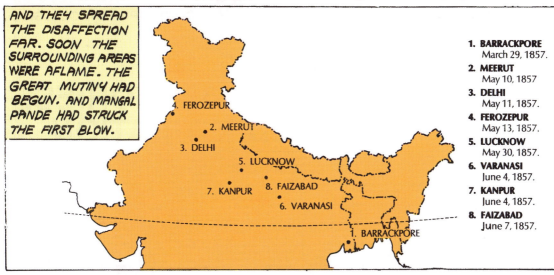

Amar Chitra Katha's

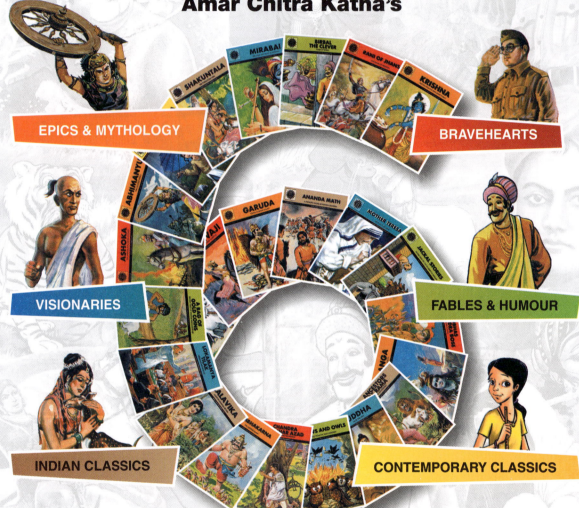

EXCITING STORY CATEGORIES, ONE AMAZING DESTINATION.

From the episodes of Mahabharata to the wit of Birbal,
from the valour of Shivaji to the teachings of Tagore,
from the adventures of Pratapan to the tales of Ruskin Bond –
Amar Chitra Katha stories span across different genres to get you the best of literature.

To buy/view our products go to